SY

WASHOE COUNTY LIBRARY

11/95

J
Mcc

D0382128

SIERRA VIEW BRANCH LIBRARY
CHILDREN'S
COLLECTION
827-0169

perty Of
Washoe County Library

DATE

SIERRA VIEW BRANCH LIBRARY
CHILDRENS LIBRARY

See You Later, Alligator

by Bobette McCarthy

Macmillan Books for Young Readers

WASHOE COUNTY LIBRARY
RENO. NEVADA

Macmillan Books for Young Readers
An imprint of Simon & Schuster Children's Publishing Division
Simon & Schuster Macmillan
1230 Avenue of the Americas
New York, New York 10020

Copyright © 1995 by Bobette McCarthy

All rights reserved including the right of reproduction
in whole or in part in any form.

Designed by Julie Y. Quan
The text of this book is set in 20 point Bookman Light.
The illustrations were done in watercolor.

Printed and bound in Singapore on recycled paper
First edition
10 9 8 7 6 5 4 3 2 1

LIBRARY OF CONGRESS CATALOGING-IN-PUBLICATION DATA
McCarthy, Bobette.
See you later, alligator / Bobette McCarthy.
p.   cm.
Summary: Playful alligators help a friend get ready to move
to a new house.
ISBN 0-02-765447-8
[1. Moving, Household—Fiction.   2. Alligators—Fiction.
3. Stories in rhyme.]   I. Title.
PZ8.3.M128Se   1995
[E]—dc20   94-19313

To Julie and Anne
and all the fun we have

See you later, Alligator.

After a while, Crocodile.

We really hate to see you move.

You have to know, we don't approve.

Don't talk like that; you'll make me cry.
It's always sad to say good-bye.
We can't stay glum; there's lots to do.
I could use an extra arm or two.

See you later, Alligator.

See you soon, you big baboon!

There's too much stuff; let's have a sale.
Hang these clothes out on a rail.

This hat, this scooter's got to go.
Someone else could use them, though.

Put a sign out on the lawn.
Before you know it, they'll be gone.

See you later, Alligator.

By and by, honey pie.

I'm getting tired, too much to pack.
I think we'd better have a snack.

I'll get the cookies and lemonade,
some nice fresh fruit and Gatorade.

Never mind, it's time to go.
I see the moving van, you know!

See you later, Alligator.

Toodle-oo, you kangaroo!

Catch you later—got to go!

Ta-ta, see you, cheerio!

Hello, Alligator! Hello, Crocodile!
Hello, everybody! Haven't seen you for a while!

Don't just stand there looking slack.
Come on, you guys, help me unpack!

WASHOE COUNTY LIBRARY
RENO, NEVADA